JODIE LANCET-GRANT

THE MARVELLOUS DOCTORS FOR MAGICAL CREATURES

From dragons with sore throats to fairies with broken wings . . .

. . . from sneezy centaurs to mermaids with measles . . .

. . . everyone in town knew exactly who to see when they were feeling poorly – Ava and her dads . . .

. . . THE MARVELLOUS DOCTORS FOR MAGICAL CREATURES

Well, Ava wasn't strictly a doctor.

Not yet.

But she *was* learning and she *loved* helping her dads in the surgery.

'This is Glitterbug,' she announced as she led in one of the unicorns who lived on Dewdrop Meadow. 'She keeps getting horrible tummy aches.'

'Oh dear,' said Daddy. 'I'm sorry to hear that. Let's take a look at you.'

Ava watched carefully as Daddy examined Glitterbug.

But he was puzzled.
He couldn't find anything wrong.

'Is something worrying you, perhaps?' he asked.
'I don't think so,' replied Glitterbug.

Ava's papa couldn't work it out either.

It was a mystery.

Luckily, Ava *loved* mysteries. And she
had a *brilliant* idea for solving this one.

'What if I spent some time with Glitterbug and tried to work out what's wrong?' she suggested. 'You know I'm excellent at searching for clues.'

'I don't see why not,' said Daddy.

'It's just as well you've been helping us out so much,' added Papa. 'You'll know just what to look out for.'

Ava beamed.
'I'll go tomorrow!'

So early the next morning, Ava set off through town to Dewdrop Meadow.

When she arrived, the unicorns were having a *wonderful* time.

All except Glitterbug, who was still feeling poorly.

Still, the herd was throwing one of their parties the next day, and getting it ready was half the fun.

Everyone was busy baking tasty treats . . .

. . . designing dramatic
dance routines . . .

. . . and making magnificent decorations
in all their favourite colours.

Ava had a marvellous day with the unicorns, but by the time dusk fell, she was no closer to solving the mystery of Glitterbug's tummy trouble.

That night she couldn't help feeling disappointed.

'You know,' said Daddy as he tucked Ava in,
'most mysteries aren't solved straight away.'

'I'll bet you'll find more
clues if you go back
tomorrow,' added Papa.

MAGIC
FIRST
AID

I ♥

Ava fell asleep, determined to try even harder the next day.

When she arrived at Dewdrop Meadow,
the party was already in full swing.

But Glitterbug was nowhere
to be seen.

YET
ANOTHER
UNICORN
PARTY !

Ava searched everywhere,

until . . .

GLITTERBUG

. . . she finally found her.

'Oh, I was just about to join the others!' she said. 'I'm so excited!'

Glitterbug did not look excited.

'Only go if you're feeling bett—' began Ava.

But before she could finish, Glitterbug had bolted back to the party.

Back at the meadow, Glitterbug joined in.
And although she was doing her best to fake it,
Ava could tell that she wasn't having fun.

As Ava watched them dance,
an idea just starting to form in
her mind, the first fat droplets
of rain began to fall.

Glitterbug frolicked around the muddy field.

She had a spring in her step and a smile on her face.

And soon,
she was almost
unrecognisable.

Ava had never seen her so happy.

It was BRILLIANT.

'How's the tummy ache?' she asked.

'It's gone!' said Glitterbug.

'I thought it might be,' said Ava.
'And I think I've worked out why.
Let's go and tell my dads!

Those colours
really suit you,
by the way.'

Back at the surgery, Ava proudly told her dads
that she had solved the mystery.

'You see, most unicorns love sunshine and sparkles
and everything pink,' Ava explained.

'And they want parties *all* the time.

But Glitterbug
isn't like that.

She prefers moody skies and storms.

She likes reading and
drawing and thinking
time on her own.

And forget pink – she
looks so cool like this.

'It's trying to fit in that's been giving Glitterbug tummy trouble. I think it will go away if she just tries to be herself!'

Glitterbug was so grateful to her new friend for solving the mystery.

'Well, looks like Ava's cracked it,' said Papa. 'And you know, there's more than one way to be a unicorn.'

'That's true,' said Daddy.

'After all, we're not exactly like other doctors, are we!'

For Eloise and Max, who are
both marvellous and magical.
J.L-G.

For my marvellous
daughter, Sylvie.
L.C.

OXFORD
UNIVERSITY PRESS

Oxford is a registered trademark
of Oxford University Press in the UK
and certain other countries

Words © Jodie Lancet-Grant, 2022
Illustrations © Lydia Corry, 2022

British Library Cataloguing
in Publication Data

Data available

ISBN: 978-0-19-277783-6

Printed in Great Britain by Bell and Bain Ltd, Glasgow

www.oup.com